Candy Soup!

A Rugrats Halloween

by Wendy Wax

illustrated by Larissa Marantz
and Shannon Bergman

Ready-to-Read

Simon Spotlight/Nickelodeon

New York   London   Toronto   Sydney

K[L][a][S]**K**[Y]
C[S]**U**[P]**O**ᵢₙ꜀.

Based on the TV series *Rugrats*® created by Arlene Klasky, Gabor Csupo, and
Paul Germain as seen on Nickelodeon®

SIMON SPOTLIGHT
An imprint of Simon & Schuster Children's Publishing Division
1230 Avenue of the Americas
New York, New York 10020

Manufactured in the United States of America
First Edition
2 4 6 8 10 9 7 5 3 1
ISBN 0-689-86832-4

Library of Congress Cataloging-in-Publication Data

Wax, Wendy.
Candy soup!: A Rugrats Halloween/by Wendy Wax; illustrated by
Larissa Marantz.—1st ed.
p. cm.— (Ready-to-read; #14)
"Based on the TV series Rugrats created by Arlene Klasky, Gabor Csupo, and
Paul Germain as seen on Nickelodeon."
Summary: Too sick to go trick-or-treating with the other Rugrats, Kimi is
allowed to eat only healthy food on Halloween, but brother Chuckie thinks of a
way for her to share their candy.
ISBN 0-689-86832-4 (pbk.)
[1. Halloween—Fiction. 2. Sick—Fiction. 3. Brothers and sisters—Fiction.
4. Soups—Fiction.] I. Marantz, Larissa, ill. II. Rugrats (Television program)
III. Title. IV. Series.
PZ7.W35117Can 2004
[E]—dc22
2004004428

"It is Halloween!" Kimi shouted,
jumping out of bed.
She put on her ghost costume and
ran to the mirror, but before
she could say "boo,"
she sneezed. "Ah-choo!"

Kimi pushed away her cereal
at breakfast. "Ah-choo! Ah-choo!"
Kira felt Kimi's head. "I think
you are getting a cold," she said.

"I want you to stay home tonight."
Kimi frowned and shook her head,
but Kira's mind was made up.

After dinner Chuckie put on his
turtle costume.
"Lucky Chuckie," Kimi said.
"I wish I could go trick-or-treating.
Ah-choo!"

"I will bring you candy," said Chuckie.
"Promise?" asked Kimi.
"Sure," said Chuckie.
"I have the best brother!" Kimi said,
 handing him her pumpkin. "You can
 put my candy in here."

"Do not bring home any candy for
Kimi," Kira said. "She needs to eat
healthy food, like soup."
Uh-oh, Chuckie had promised
Kimi he would!

The doorbell rang.
"Trick or treat!" yelled Angelica.
Kira gave out boxes of jelly beans.
"Have fun," she called as Chuckie
left with the group.

"Where is Kimi?" Susie asked. "Home," said Chuckie. "My mommy says she is too sick to eat candy." "But candy makes people feel better," said Angelica, popping a jelly bean into her mouth.

They went to the house next door
and rang the doorbell. A magician
opened the door.
"I will give you a trick and a treat,"
he said. He waved a wand over
a hat and pulled out lollipops.
Angelica grabbed a red one.

"Kimi likes purple lollies," said Lil.
"But all she gets is soup," said
    Chuckie.

"Hey, Chuckie," said Tommy.
"Maybe you can sneak some candy
to Kimi."
"I do not want to get in trouble,"
Chuckie said.

"Scaredy turtle!" Angelica teased.
Chuckie hung his head. He did not
know what to do.

The babies went to the next house.
A skeleton opened the door
and passed out bottles of water.
"This is not candy!" Angelica cried.
"Candy is bad for your teeth," said
the skeleton. "It made mine fall out."

16

It started to get dark.

"I am thirsty," Angelica said.

She handed her water bottle to Drew,
and he opened it for her.

Angelica took a sip. Then she
dropped it back in her pumpkin.

At the next house they got
mints from a ghost.
"Who is splashing me?" Angelica
asked.
"You are," Tommy said.
Angelica peeked in her pumpkin.

"My water spilled!" she cried.
"Now I have wet candy."
"Look! Candy soup!" said Tommy.
"We can give it to Kimi! My mommy
said she could eat soup!" said Chuckie.
Everyone liked that idea.

They dumped the candy soup
into Kimi's pumpkin.
Angelica took out her candy.
"You can not do that!" said Susie.
"Candy soup needs candy."
"Put your own candy in," Angelica
said, stuffing her pockets.

"Put your purple lolly in the soup, Lil!" said Phil.
"But I want to eat my purple lolly," said Lil. Instead she dropped in a broken candy bar.
Tommy took a taste. "It needs more candy," he said.

21

Chuckie pulled a string out of the soup. "What is this?" he asked. "A candy necklace," said Angelica. "I hope Kimi does not mind that I bit the candy off." "She will not," said Susie, adding the candy she did not like.

At the house across from Chuckie's,
a woman handed out bags
of fish crackers.
"The fishies can swim in the soup!"
Tommy said.
Plip. Plip. Plip. Everyone dropped
them in.

Kimi's pumpkin got too heavy
for Chuckie to carry alone.
"We will all carry it in together,"
said Lil.
"Good idea," said Tommy.
"Mommy and Kimi will be happy,"
said Chuckie.

Kira was busy giving out candy.
"Be with you in a minute,"
she called to the babies.
They met Kimi in the living room.

"Candy!" Kimi shouted.
But when she looked inside
the pumpkin, she was sad.
"Taste it, Kimi," said Phil.
Lil handed her the spoon.

"What is this?" Kimi asked.

"Candy soup!" said Chuckie.

"We made it for you."

"With mints, purple lollies,
 and gumdrops?" Kimi asked.

"Not exactly," said Phil.

"Yuck," Kimi said after tasting it.

"We should have used better candy,"
 mumbled Chuckie.

Then Kira came into the room.
"What is going on? Is that candy?"
She looked at Chuckie.
"It is candy soup," said Angelica.
"Candy soup?" Kira said with a
frown.

"Chuckie, I told you not to bring Kimi candy," said Kira.

"But we made it into soup so
Kimi would feel better," said Susie.
Kira sighed.
"I guess you babies meant well,"
she said, smiling.

Kira let Kimi have one piece
of candy. She chose a purple lolly,
and as soon as she ate it,
she felt much better!